To my mother, who likes polka dots   D. D.

To John Werner, a snappy dresser who didn't mind
mixing plaid with polka dots   J. M.

First edition 2002

Library of Congress Cataloging-in-Publication Data

Dodds, Dayle Ann.
The Kettles get new clothes / Dayle Ann Dodds ; illustrated by Jill McElmurry. —1st ed.
p.   cm.
Summary: When the small store where they usually buy their clothes changes hands, the Kettles
are in for a surprise on their annual shopping trip.
ISBN 0-7636-1091-7
[1. Clothing and dress—Fiction. 2. Shopping—Fiction.] I. McElmurry, Jill, ill. II. Title.
PZ7.D66285 Ke 2002
[E]—dc21   00-049373

10 9 8 7 6 5 4 3 2 1

Printed in China

This book was typeset in Clichee.
The illustrations were done in gouache.

Candlewick Press
2067 Massachusetts Avenue
Cambridge, Massachusetts 02140

visit us at www.candlewick.com

The Kettles Get New Clothes

Dayle Ann Dodds

ILLUSTRATED BY Jill McElmurry

CANDLEWICK PRESS
CAMBRIDGE, MASSACHUSETTS

Once a year, every year, the Kettles got new clothes.

Father Kettle, Mother Kettle, Sister, Brother, and Baby Kettle went to the little shop in the city to buy brand-new clothes, plain and simple as you please.

But one year things changed. When the Kettles arrived at the shop, they were met with a surprise. Where there once was a small wooden door, there now stood a tall, shiny glass door, with sparkling handles trimmed in gold.

As they reached for the door, someone rushed to greet them.

"Bonjour!" said Monsieur Pip. "You are in need of new clothes? You have come to the right place. My customers are always happy.

"G-U-A-R-A-N-T-E-E-D!"

Before the Kettles could say a word, Monsieur Pip pulled out his tape and measured each one, top to bottom. Snip, snap.

"Follow me!" said Monsieur Pip,
heading for the dressing rooms.
"I have exactly what you need!"

DRESSING ROOMS

SO THE KETTLES WENT IN . . .

and the Kettles came out.

"PAISLEY," said Monsieur Pip,
"is perky and spry. I love it, don't you?
Just give it a try."

But the Kettles weren't so sure.

"Too perky," said Father.
"Too spry," said Mother.
"Don't love it," said Sister.
"Nor I!" said Brother.

Only Baby smiled.

"PAISLEY is not for everyone," said Monsieur Pip. "But do not worry. I have something else. Follow me!"

SO THE KETTLES WENT IN . . .

and the Kettles came out.

"STRIPES," said Monsieur Pip, "are forceful and strong. The perfect choice all along!"

But the Kettles weren't so sure.

"Too forceful," said Father.
"Too strong," said Mother.
"Not perfect," said Sister.
"Just wrong!" said Brother.

Only Baby smiled.

"Of course, STRIPES are not for everyone," grumbled Monsieur Pip, patting his brow with his handkerchief. "But do not worry. I have something else. Follow me."

SO THE KETTLES WENT IN . . .

and the Kettles came out.

"CHECKS," said Monsieur Pip,
"are cheery and snappy. I'm CERTAIN that
these will make you happy."

But the Kettles weren't so sure.

"Too cheery," said Father.
"Too snappy," said Mother.
"Not certain," said Sister.
"Not HAPPY!" said Brother.

Only Baby smiled.

"Perhaps CHECKS are not for everyone," snarled Monsieur Pip, gritting his teeth. "But do not worry. I have something else. Follow me."

SO THE KETTLES WENT IN . . .

and the Kettles came out.

"DOTS," growled Monsieur Pip, "are playful and fun. Dots are a favorite of EVERYONE."

But the Kettles weren't so sure.

"Too playful," said Father.
"Too fun," said Mother.
"No favorite," said Sister.
"I'm DONE!" said Brother.

Only Baby smiled.

"Mon dieu," Monsieur Pip sobbed.

"That's it! I have NO new clothes for the Kettles, G-U-A-R-A-N-T-E-E-D. You are not happy. I am not happy. Oh, I am a failure!"

"We're sorry," said the Kettles. "We just wanted some new clothes, plain and simple as you please." They offered Monsieur Pip a handkerchief.

"Plain and simple?" said Monsieur Pip, dabbing his eyes. "Why didn't you say so? If it's plain and simple you want, it's plain and simple you shall have! Follow me."

AND SO, THE KETTLES WENT IN . . .

and then the Kettles came out.

Monsieur Pip held his breath.

DRESSING
ROOMS

"Spunky!" said Father.

"Snappy!" said Mother.

"Cheery!" said Sister.

"HAPPY!" said Brother.

"YES!" said Monsieur Pip,
  sinking to the floor in relief.

  Only Baby was crying.

"Could it be," said Monsieur Pip, with hopeful anticipation, "you want something MORE?"

Monsieur Pip leaped up at the thought, singing and dancing around his shop, his heart filled with glee.

"Follow me!" said Monsieur Pip.

SO BABY WENT IN . . .

and Baby came out.

"Perfect!" they all shouted.

"Of course," said Monsieur Pip,
"I had no doubt, for my customers
are ALWAYS happy."

"GUARANTEED!"